The Klondike Cat

WRITTEN BY Julie LAWSON

ILLUSTRATED BY Paul MOMBOURQUETTE

Kids Can Press

GOLD IN THE KLONDIKE!
NUGGETS THE SIZE OF A MAN'S FIST!

The news spread like flames in a summer wind. From house to house, city to city, coast to coast, *everyone* was catching gold fever.

And one day, Noah's father caught it, too.

"Start packing, son!" Pa said. "Come March, we're heading north."

Noah's eyes widened. "Both of us?"

"I need your help," said Pa.

"Shadow can help, too!"

"No, lad." Pa gave the cat her favorite scratch beneath the chin. "Shadow has to stay home with Aunty."

"Please, Pa! She won't be any trouble."

"No," Pa repeated. "I'm sorry."

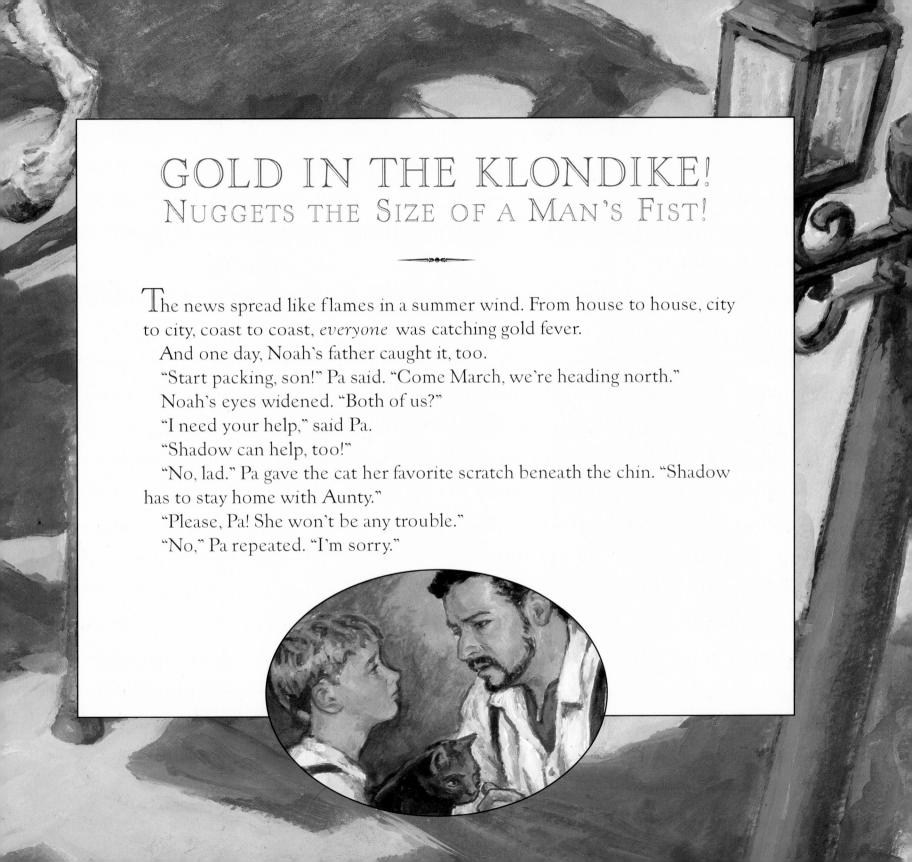

The weeks flew by.

Noah grew more and more excited as he helped Pa prepare for the journey. But how could he leave Shadow? "She knows we're going away, Pa," he said. "She follows me everywhere. Please let her come!"

"No," Pa said firmly. "The journey's too long and too hard." And no amount of pleading would change his mind.

———◆———

The day of their departure finally arrived. "Oh, Shadow!" Noah cried. "What'll I do without you?"

Shadow twined herself around his legs and purred.

Right then and there, Noah made up his mind. He opened his pack, removed a sweater and tucked Shadow inside. "You have to be quiet," he whispered.

Shadow gave a forlorn meow. But to Noah's relief, she stayed quiet and still all the way to the harbor.

The wharf was packed.

"Is the whole *world* going to the Klondike?" Noah gasped.

Men shouted. Horses neighed. Dogs barked.

As Shadow squirmed and scratched to get out, Noah tightened his hold on the bulging pack. If Pa found out now ...

Pa didn't seem to notice. He strode up the gangplank, located their cabin and chose their berths. "We're on our way, Noah," he said. "Coming out on deck to wave good-bye?"

"In a minute." Noah eyed his pack nervously.

The instant Pa left, Noah opened the pack, scooped up Shadow and gave her a hug. "Good cat!" he said.

Suddenly, the steamboat whistle shrieked. With a startled yowl, Shadow leapt from Noah's arms and bolted out the door.

"Come back!" Noah cried. He ran down the corridor after her, but she was too fast. Choking back tears, he searched the ship from bow to stern, desperately calling her name. But Shadow had disappeared.

The ship steamed up the coast.

With each passing day, Noah grew more anxious. Where was Shadow?

After six days at sea, the ship entered a narrow canal. Excitement swelled to a frenzy. When the ship dropped anchor, stampeders began jumping into the lifeboats. "Klondike, ho!" they cheered.

"Now the *real* journey begins," Pa said.

Noah's stomach churned. How could he leave the ship without Shadow?

Just then, a crewman came up from the hold. "Anybody want this cat? Dandy mouser, but we've already got one."

Shadow! Noah's heart pounded.

"No takers?" the crewman said. "Well then, it's over the side."

"Stop!" Noah cried. "She's mine!" He scrambled across the deck and gathered Shadow into his arms. "It's all right," he murmured.

Or was it? He caught his father's eye and slowly walked toward him. "I'm sorry, Pa," he said. "I couldn't leave her behind."

Pa gave him a long, hard look, then said sternly, "The minute she proves trouble, she's got to go."

"She'll be good," Noah promised. "And I'll work hard enough for both of us."

The work began the moment they stepped on shore. The beach was awash with sacks and crates of provisions. They had to find their goods, then haul them above the high-water line in a frantic race against the tide. Twenty trips it took, one hundred pounds at a time.

It was well after dark when they set up their tent and collapsed in their sleeping bags.

"Night, son," Pa said. "You worked mighty hard today." He patted Noah's head and, almost at once, began to snore.

Outside, the wind shook the canvas walls, and the flickering of thousands of candles cast shadows throughout the tent city.

Noah hugged Shadow. "It's *almost* like home," he whispered. "And if you're good, Shadow, you can stay."

The next morning, Pa said, "This is it, son! All set for the Chilkoot Trail?"

"Yes, sir!" Noah grinned.

The days soon took on a rhythm. Load up in the morning, hike the rugged trail, cache the load and return to camp before dusk. Each day ended with a supper of beans and bacon, or pea soup and flapjacks, washed down with a mug of tea.

Noah always saved Shadow a bit of evaporated cream. Pa sometimes gave her a piece of bacon. But she hunted her own meals.

"See?" Noah said as Shadow dropped a mouse at Pa's feet. "She's no trouble." Then, remembering how Pa had tripped over Shadow the day before, he added, "She's been good ... hasn't she, Pa?"

Pa grunted.

When the last load was hauled, they set up a new camp and another cache and moved on to the next stage. Back and forth they went, through rain and slush and mud and snow, cold and tired and sore.

———◦———

"When will we get there?" Noah asked one night. His feet hurt and his muscles ached. "Pa? It's been one month already. How much farther?"

Pa didn't answer. "You're shivering," he said, rummaging through Noah's pack. "Where's your heavy sweater?"

"I left it behind to make room for Shadow." Then, seeing Pa scowl, he added, "It's not her fault. And I'm not really cold."

Pa grunted. He removed his own sweater, pulled it over Noah's head, and tucked him into his sleeping bag. "Rest up, lad. We've still got a long way to go."

The steep, icy climb to the Chilkoot Summit was hard on Shadow's paws. When she began to limp, Noah carried her in his pack or tucked her inside his coat.

The other stampeders laughed. "At least a dog can pull a sled. Is that cat pullin' its weight?"

"Well ..." Noah hesitated.

"No mice in our food supplies," Pa said. "Isn't that right, son?"

Noah's face lit up. Shadow could stay!

At the end of April, they reached Bennett Lake.

It was still frozen, but another rush was on — to build a boat before the ice broke.

Noah helped Pa as best he could and, by the middle of May, their boat was taking shape. What's more, the days were long and sunny and the snow was melting. Noah's spirits were high.

But Shadow was acting strangely. Restless and whiny. In the tent and out of the tent. And pernickety! Even when Noah offered her a tasty morsel of bacon, she turned up her nose. She was awfully fat for a pernickety cat. And now she'd been gone for a week.

What was wrong with Shadow?

One morning in late May, Noah heard a thunderous crack. The ice on the lake was breaking.

"Next stop, Dawson City!" Pa said. "Start packing, Noah."

Noah raced back to camp. Socks and towels off the wash line ... He stopped abruptly. A faint stirring was coming from the tent. He went inside, peeked behind a stack of crates, and discovered four bright-eyed kittens.

At that moment, Shadow squirmed under the canvas carrying another kitten. She glanced up at Noah, then stretched out while the kittens snuggled against her.

"Oh, Shadow!" Noah smiled with delight. "So that's what you've been up to!" Then his smile faded. Pa would never let him keep the kittens. Unless ...

"Shadow," he said, "if your kittens are quiet and don't cause any trouble, they can stay. Otherwise, they'll have to go."

He found the perfect hiding place in a crate of woolen blankets and moved the kittens, one by one, under Shadow's watchful eye.

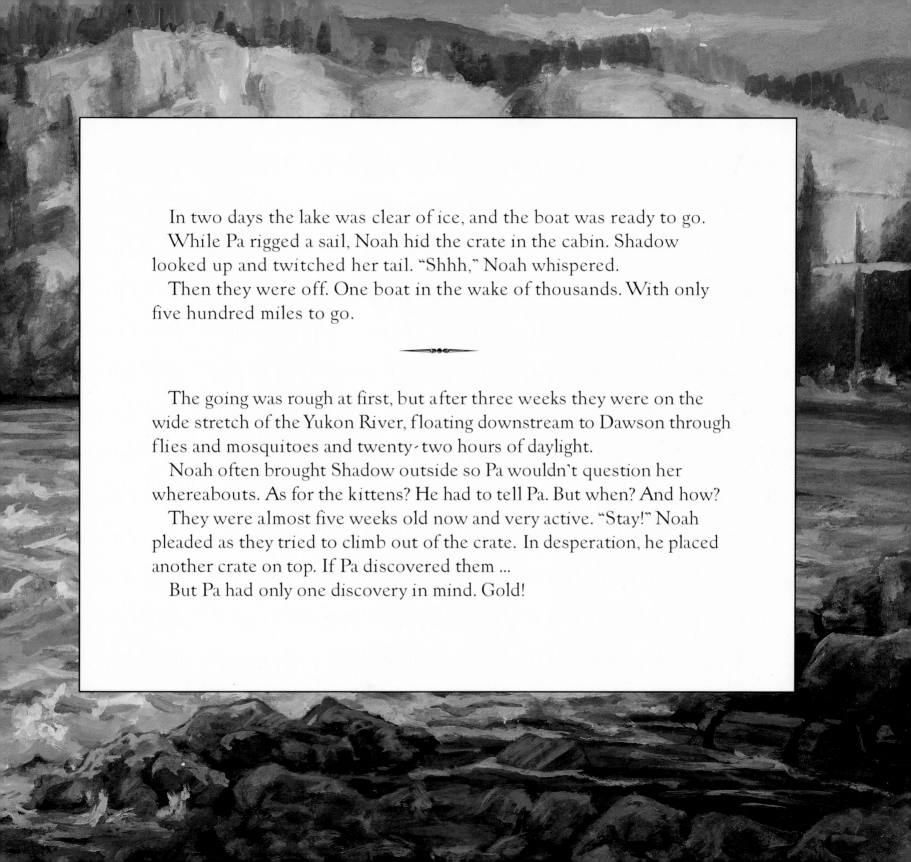

In two days the lake was clear of ice, and the boat was ready to go.

While Pa rigged a sail, Noah hid the crate in the cabin. Shadow looked up and twitched her tail. "Shhh," Noah whispered.

Then they were off. One boat in the wake of thousands. With only five hundred miles to go.

The going was rough at first, but after three weeks they were on the wide stretch of the Yukon River, floating downstream to Dawson through flies and mosquitoes and twenty-two hours of daylight.

Noah often brought Shadow outside so Pa wouldn't question her whereabouts. As for the kittens? He had to tell Pa. But when? And how?

They were almost five weeks old now and very active. "Stay!" Noah pleaded as they tried to climb out of the crate. In desperation, he placed another crate on top. If Pa discovered them ...

But Pa had only one discovery in mind. Gold!

One day, as the boat swept around a bluff, Noah saw a rough-and-tumble city sprawled out along the river. He gaped. "Is that Dawson?"

"Yessir!" Pa whooped. "We made it!"

"Pa, about Shadow ..."

"Later, son. You stay with our goods. I'm off to get us a gold claim."

Noah couldn't wait to let out the kittens. He laughed as they tumbled and frolicked about. He was so caught up in the fun he lost all track of time.

———✦———

"NOAH!"

He jumped. And when he saw Pa's expression, he feared the worst.

Then, unexpectedly, Pa slumped onto a crate and buried his face in his hands. "We're too late," he said. "All the good land is staked. A few claims are for sale but we can't afford to buy one. We don't have enough money. We may have to turn around and go home. And Noah ... these kittens have got to go. I'll take another look around and think some more. But when I come back ..."

Noah nodded sadly.

"Oh, Shadow!" Noah moaned. "We can't have come all this way for nothing. There must be something we can do."

He hurried into Dawson to look for himself. The streets swarmed with newcomers trying to sell their goods. Wealthy prospectors mingled about, too. They'd come in from the goldfields and were looking for something special, like an egg or a tin of tomatoes. Noah wished he had what they wanted.

He listened to the prospectors talking about the winter they'd spent alone in their cabins with only the mice for company. And right then and there, he had an idea.

He ran to the boat and printed a sign. Then he put Shadow and the kittens in a crate and raced back to town.

A crowd gathered around him. "I'll give you five dollars for a kitten!" one prospector shouted.

"Make it ten!" cried another.

A third called out, "I'll give you an ounce of gold!"

"Sold!" Noah beamed. An ounce of gold — why, that was sixteen dollars!

Within minutes, he'd sold all five kittens. "Wait till we tell Pa!" he said and gave Shadow a hug.

Pa was waiting at the boat. When Noah handed him the gold, Pa stared in amazement. For a long time, he didn't speak. Finally, he cleared his throat and said, "Noah, lad. This will make all the difference. You and Shadow — you've done me proud."

Noah felt ten feet tall.

That night, as they crawled into their sleeping bags, Pa said, "Sleep well, son. Tomorrow we're off to the goldfields. And I reckon we might stay put for a while."

"All three of us?" Noah asked.

"Yessir!" Pa smiled and ruffled Noah's hair.

For a long time, Noah lay awake. He thought of their long journey and all the nights they'd spent on the trail. What would it be like to stay put for a while?

Well, one thing was certain. As long as he had Shadow's purrs on one side and Pa's snores on the other, it would feel like home.